This book is given to:

_____

from:

_____

Dedication

To Strong Tower Bible Church,
a ColorFull display of God's diverse kingdom,
full of kind thoughts, and showered with grace.
You truly are the heart behind these stories.

Copyright © 2019 by B&H Publishing Group

All rights reserved.

978-1-4627-9284-9

Published by B&H Publishing Group,
Nashville, Tennessee

All Scripture quotations are taken from the Christian
Standard Bible®, Copyright © 2017 by Holman Bible Publishers.
Used by permission. Christian Standard Bible® and CSB® are
federally registered trademarks of Holman Bible Publishers.

DEWEY: C234.1   SBHD: GRACE (THEOLOGY) / HOMELESSNESS / POVERTY

Printed in October 2018 in Shenzhen, Guangdong, China

1 2 3 4 5 6 · 23 22 21 20 19

GraceFull

Growing a Heart That Cares for Our Neighbors

Dorena Williamson

Illustrated by Geneva B

B&H
PUBLISHING GROUP
Nashville, Tennessee

On Sunday morning, the church was filled with joyful music. Hope and her family clapped and sang along.

"Good morning!" said Pastor Will to welcome everyone. "I'm so glad to see you all in God's house today! It's time for our monthly grace offering. Our gifts will lift someone up, just as God has done for us.

"This month's grace offering will help the Habib family get back on their feet. They are staying at The Chen House, where our church will be volunteering this week."

Leaving church, Hope told her parents about her new friend, Anna Habib, whose family was from Syria.

"Mom, when Pastor Will talked about the Habib family, what did he mean, 'They're getting back on their feet'?"

"Well, right now their family is homeless," replied her mom.

"You mean they don't have a home? I thought the pastor said they are living at a chin house!" said Hope.

"I'm glad you were listening!" said Mom. "The Habib family went through some hard times and lost their home. The Chen House is a shelter where homeless families live while they look for a better job and a new home."

WILL WORK FOR FOOD

"What's it like there?" asked Hope.
"How about we go volunteer with the church and see for ourselves?" said Mom.

On volunteer day, Hope wasn't sure what to expect, but she smiled when she saw Anna talking with their friend Ahanu.

"Hi, Hope! We get to work in the garden together!" greeted Anna.
"And we might find a worm!" said Ahanu with a big smile.

"Really? Are you sure there's a garden *here?*" asked Hope, looking at the concrete sidewalks and walls of the city.

Anna leaned in to whisper. "It's a secret garden. On the roof!"

The kids ran up the stairs, and Hope was so surprised at what she found. . . .

"Wow! I never thought all this would be growing way up here! It's so colorful!"

"Yes, it is!" said Ms. Habib. "Even better, the veggies from this roof help feed families like us who stay here. And money from selling extra vegetables helps too."

"And it feeds the worms!" Ahanu grinned.

"All that gardening sure made me hungry.
I'm glad it started raining so we could stop for lunch!" said Anna.
"And I'm glad you're eating your vegetables!" laughed Ms. Habib.

"We better get home," said Hope's mom, "but we'll see you for dinner at our house tomorrow night. More veggies, but no worms," she added with a wink.

Hope spent the next morning in the garden at home. "Did you like helping at The Chen House yesterday?" asked her mom.

"Yes. But it doesn't seem fair that the Habibs have to live in a shelter," said Hope.

"You're right. It's not fair. But I am glad to know places like The Chen House, and our church, can help show God's grace. Hopefully with Ms. Habib's new job, their family will get a place of their own soon."

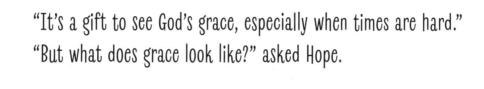

"It's a gift to see God's grace, especially when times are hard."
"But what does grace look like?" asked Hope.

Mom thought for a second. "Well, kind of like the rain. Every good gift is from above, Hope. God showers blessings on all of us. When we truly understand that, we can't help but share grace and lift others up. Much like how the rain makes this rosebush grow full of flowers we can then share. When grace is full and overflowing, we are graceFull!"

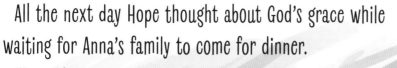

All the next day Hope thought about God's grace while waiting for Anna's family to come for dinner.

"Anna, let's go to my room. I've got some new rain boots you can have if they fit you!"

"They fit! Are you sure I can have them?" asked Anna.

"Sure! Mom said that God showers blessings on us to share with others."

"Wow, thanks! I can't wait to wear them the next time it rains!" said Anna.

It was a joyful day when the Habib family moved to a home of their own. Hope and her family came by to celebrate.

"We're so happy for you!" said Hope's mom as she hugged Ms. Habib.

"And we wanted to share this rosebush with you so you can grow something colorful in your own backyard," said Hope's dad.

"That's so thoughtful. You all have been such a blessing to us!" said Grandma Habib.

"Anna, I like your new house!"
said Hope.

"Thanks!" said Anna. "Mama says
God's grace just keeps falling on us."

"Well, a little *more* grace might be falling. . .
it looks like rain!" said Hope. "Let's go see."

Anna stretched her hands out to catch the raindrops.
"It's showers of *blessing*!" she said.
"Yep!" said Hope, "and thanks to God, we're grace*Full*!"

Remember:

"May the Lord bless you and protect you; may the Lord make his face shine on you and be gracious to you; may the Lord look with favor on you and give you peace."—Numbers 6:24-26

Read:

Read 2 Corinthians 8:1-15. Paul was an apostle who started many churches and wrote letters that became books in the Bible. In this letter, he tells about one church that had gone through hard times. Although the people had very little, God's grace moved their hearts to be generous in helping others. Another church was strong in faith and knowledge, but they needed to grow in the grace of giving. They had plenty and could help those who had less.

Paul reminds us that Jesus left the riches of heaven's glory to be born a poor baby. Because of His sacrifice, we get to receive the riches of salvation by grace. Jesus' example of empowering the powerless is what we should follow. Everything we have has been given to us by God, and we grow by giving to others. Then we will be full and overflowing with grace—GraceFull!

Think:

1. In this story, the church collects a grace offering to lift up Anna's family. Where do you find opportunities to help others?

2. Hope and Anna are friends at church. How are their families the same? How are they different?

3. Anna's family has to live in a shelter for a while. Some homeless people live on the street. How would you want to be treated if you were homeless? Why?

4. The homeless shelter is called The Chen House. *Chen* is a Hebrew word that means "grace." How does grace make families at The Chen House feel? Why?

5. In the story, grace is in the worship song about God's favor, in the rain that showers down, and in the flowers that grow and are given as a gift. How does God show grace to you? How can you share it with others?